Second Chance Wolf

The Bite-Sized Shifters Series
By
Rose Bak

Second Chance Wolf

Bite-Sized Shifters, Volume 7

Rose Bak

Published by Rose Bak, 2022.

Also by Rose Bak

Bite-Sized Shifters
Long Distance Wolf
Wolf Doctor
Kat's Dog
Designer Wolf
Wolf Sheriff
Cocktail Wolf
Second Chance Wolf

Boozy Book Club
Beach Reads
Bubbly & Billionaires: A Midlife Instalove Romantic Comedy
Martinis & Mysteries

Diamond Bay
Brand New Penny
Fresh as a Daisy
Right as Rain

Good With Numbers
Love Unmasked
The Thanksgiving Scrooge
Maid for Christmas
Countdown to Love
Valentine's Lottery

Holidays With the Shifters
Santa's Claws
Bear Humbug
Jingle Bear
Joy to the Wolf
Lion's Heart
Silver Paws

Loving the Holidays
Dating Santa
New Year's Steve
Independence Dave

Magical Midlife Romance
Love Potion

Oliver Boys Band

Until You Came Along
Rock Star Teacher
Rock Star Writer
Rock Star Neighbor
Rock Star Lawyer

Reunited
Together Again
Finding My Baby

Self-Help for the Real World
It's All About Relationships

Standalone
What to Do If You Find a Cougar in Your Living Room
Beach Wedding
Good with Numbers
Christmas Love Stories: A Holiday Romance Anthology
Diamond Bay
Christmas with the Shifters

Watch for more at https://rosebakenterprises.com/.

Table of Contents

About This Book

He let her go once, but there's no way he's letting his mate get away a second time.

Thirty years ago, wolf shifter Damon met his true mate. Unfortunately, he was already married to someone else, with a baby on the way. Letting Angie go was the hardest thing he ever did, but he always knew that somehow fate would bring them together again.

Angie is only back in the shifter town of Greysden long enough to mend fences with her sister and help settle their parents' estate. She has no desire to stay in the town where she experienced so much loss, even if her sister's new neighbor is her long-lost mate. Too much time has passed, and they're both too old for this mate nonsense, right?

With a little help from her matchmaking family, Damon is going to show Angie that second chances are precious, and midlife love is worth taking a chance on...

"Second Chance Wolf" is book seven in the "Bite-Sized Shifters" series, a series of paranormal romantic comedies you can read in just a few hours. Each book in the series is a standalone featuring a mature couple, steamy scenes, a lot of fur and claws, and a guaranteed HEA.

This book includes a special excerpt from "Wolf Doctor", book one of the Bite-Sized Shifters series, available now from all major online retailers.

Be sure to join Rose's mailing list and get a free book. Click here[1] to be the first to hear about all the latest releases and special sales.

---

1. https://storyoriginapp.com/giveaways/62ee758e-068f-11eb-904e-c373f6014fe1

Dedication

For everyone who wonders "what if" when they think about their first love.

Angie

"We're going to need more lube."

I repressed a sigh as James slicked up his cock and went back in. He'd been pumping into me for what felt like thirty-seven hours, and he still hadn't reached his orgasm. I wondered if he had a medical issue. I mean, I appreciated a guy with some longevity, but this was ridiculous. Meanwhile any arousal I felt was long gone. I needed him to finish and leave so I could take care of myself.

James stiffened above me and finally came with a long groan. *Thank the gods,* I thought.

Deep inside me, my wolf woke up from her nap. She flicked her tail dismissively, unimpressed with my boyfriend's sexual prowess. My other half never liked it when I slept with men who weren't my fated mate. Most wolf shifters believed that fate would send them the perfect mate, and that had happened for me too. Unfortunately, things hadn't worked out with our mate, but the animal was too simple to understand the complexities of human relationships.

I pushed my mate out of my mind as James rolled off me, flopping on his back and breathing heavily. He turned his head and pressed a string of sweet kisses along my neck.

"That was incredible, baby."

Gah. I hated it when men called me 'baby'. I didn't like it when I was twenty and I liked it even less at fifty. I also didn't appreciate his complete disinterest in making sure I was satisfied when we slept together. Spoiler alert: I never was.

I pulled the blanket up to my neck and stared at the ceiling, wondering if I should break up with James. I guess I should tell him that we were better as friends. He was an interesting guy, and it was nice having a date for events, but the sex was so lackluster that I almost always wound up finishing myself off with my vibrator after he left – if I had the energy.

I heard a soft snore as James started to fall asleep. Damn it, I'd told him a hundred times I didn't like people sleeping over. I pushed on his shoulder.

"Wake up James, time to go."

My boyfriend grumbled, but finally got up and got dressed. I practically pushed him out the door, not even allowing him to linger for a kiss. I stalked back to my bedroom, assessing whether I was in the mood to pull out my vibrator and finish what James started. I was leaning towards just going to sleep.

My phone buzzed as I crossed the living room. I detoured to the table where it was attached to a charging cord. *Connie.* I frowned. I hadn't heard from my older sister in several months. She didn't usually call unless something was up. I felt a twinge of sadness, remembering how close we were before everything happened.

"Hey Connie," I greeted. "Is everything okay?"

My sister sniffed. "It's Mom. She's gone. The doctor thinks it was a heart attack."

I sank to the floor as my legs gave out. "No," I whispered, surprised by how upset I was at the death of a parent I hadn't talked to in years.

"How's Dad?" I asked grudgingly. I hoped he'd be burning in hell soon, just like my mother.

"I don't think he's going to make it," she sobbed. "He's just laying in the bed, cradling Mom, howling and refusing to let them take the body. You've got to come home, Angie."

"But..."

"Please. I know how you feel about Greysden, I know how you feel about Dad, but I need you Angie." Her voice broke. "I can't do this alone, I need my sister."

Unlike me, Connie had maintained a relationship with our parents. I, on the other hand, hadn't seen or talked to my parents since I was eighteen. She was much more forgiving than me, and I know she'd wanted her son to have a relationship with his grandparents. It stung a little that Connie had kept them in her life while I was all the way out here, all alone. But then again, she wasn't the one they'd tried to...I pushed the thought out of my mind.

I had no desire to go back but I couldn't deny my sister; she never asked me for anything. I took a deep shuddering breath.

"OK Connie. I'm going to drive; airfares will be ridiculous with this short of notice. I'll leave in the morning."

"Thanks Sis, see you soon."

After a mostly sleepless night I was up with the sun. Or as much sun as we got in Seattle at this time of the year. Pulling on some loose sweats, I walked a couple of blocks over to a trailhead. I needed to run my wolf before we headed out on our long drive, or she would drive me crazy. She hated being cooped up in the car. After checking to make sure there were no humans around, I pulled off my clothes and hid them between some rocks.

Once I was naked I stretched my arms over my head, loosening up my spine, and took a deep breath. I exhaled, calling my wolf forward. There was a brief flash of pain as my bones broke and lengthened, and my muscles and tendons grew. I fell to all fours as fur sprouted all over my body and a tail extended from my spine. Claws and fangs dropped last.

My wolf shook herself and then took off at a slow amble. We weren't as young as we used to be, and I could feel my wolf slowing down a bit, but she still loved to chase rabbits and chipmunks like she was a pup. It was a beautiful morning to run, misty but warm.

As I ran through the woods, I thought of the last time I was in Greysden. The last time I saw my family. How my parents betrayed me for money. And then I thought of him. Damon. My true mate. Fate was a cruel bitch, because although she brought us together, Damon and I were doomed to be apart. I urged my wolf to run faster, to wipe the memories out of my mind.

This was going to be a hard trip. I only hoped I could get through it as painlessly as possible so I could return to Seattle and never set foot in Greysden again.

Damon

"Dad, are you sure about this?"

I looked over at my daughter with a fond smile. "Yeah sweetie, I am."

"I don't understand. You've lived in Denver for thirty years. You love Denver. Why are you going to move to some little town in the middle of nowhere?"

"I grew up near Greysden," I reminded her. "That area is home for me."

Home is wherever our mate is, my wolf grumbled in mind. *We have to find her.*

I felt a stab of pain as Angie's face flashed in my memory. My best friend's little sister. Well, sister-in-law. Andy had mated with and married Angie's older sister, Connie. I'd been the best man and eighteen-year-old Angie had been the maid of honor. The minute I set eyes on her for the first time at the wedding rehearsal dinner I knew. Angie was my fated mate.

At the time I'd felt the most incredible rush of joy. It was every shifter's dream: to find the one person in all the world who was perfect for them. The other half of your soul. My wolf had gone crazy with excitement.

Unfortunately, it wasn't meant to be. I wasn't free. I was already married and had a pregnant wife. It was a no-win situation: be with my mate and betray my wife, or be with my wife and betray my mate.

Angie and I had shared one kiss. One incredible kiss that I'd relived every day of my life since then. One kiss that confirmed two things: we were fated mates and we could not be together, no matter how much either of us wished things were different.

The day after the wedding Angie was gone. As far as I knew, she'd never set a paw in Greysden again. Andy had been close-mouthed about what happened to his sister-in-law, and I never asked. It was too painful.

I'd moved away not long after that, living in Denver with my human wife and our kids. When my kids were little I always imagined that I'd go find my mate when they graduated high school. But that time came and went, years ago now, and I was ashamed to admit that I let inertia keep me in place long after my kids were grown and my wife was dead.

Lately though, Angie was in my thoughts again. Maybe it was weird for me to move back to Greysden, but I'd been dreaming of Angie every night for months. Long, vivid dreams of the two of us frolicking through the woods, living in Greysden. I couldn't help but wonder if it was a premonition of some kind. Something was calling me home, and I was determined to follow my instincts.

"I'm really going to miss you, Dad."

I wrapped my daughter into a hug. "I know, but you're almost thirty, married and settled down, just like your sister. And I've been working since I was a kid. I'm ready to retire."

"I can't believe you're retiring at fifty-five," she grumbled. "You're so lucky."

"I'll still be doing some consulting work to keep busy, and I'll be close enough that I can come up for the kids' birthdays and special events. You'll hardly even notice I'm gone."

That part was true. My girls were all grown up with families of their own. They didn't have a lot of time for their dear old dad, and with their mother gone for ten years now, they were pretty self-sufficient. I'd done my job with them. I'd raised them, provided for them, sent them through college. And I'd stayed married to a woman who wasn't my mate, a woman I didn't love, all so they could live in a two-parent household. I'd literally sacrificed my happiness for them. But now my work was done. It was time for me.

I had no idea where my mate had ended up after she'd left Greysden, but my wolf and I were in agreement: we needed to be there in case she came back. If my dreams were right, she would come back, if she wasn't there already.

Pulling away from my daughter, I headed towards my SUV. It was stuffed with suitcases and some things I didn't want to entrust with the movers. As I headed towards the road that would lead me to Greysden, I felt lighter than I had in years.

It's time, my wolf whispered. *We've waited for our mate long enough.*

Angie

"Thanks for coming, sis."

My sister enveloped me in a warm hug, and I clung to her, fighting tears. I'd purposely distanced myself from her over the years, yet the minute we were together it was like no time had passed.

"I've really missed you," I whispered, realizing it was true.

Why had I stayed away so long? The drama with my father was way in the past and while I was still angry and hurt about it, I'd been a self-sufficient adult for a long time. He had no control over me. No one did. I could have made an effort to visit my sister and her family and still avoided seeing my parents.

Connie pulled me into the house, and I looked around curiously, taking in the comfortable space. I'd never been here before, but I knew she and her mate Andy had lived here for many years, raising their son in this house.

"How about some coffee?" she suggested.

I followed Connie into the kitchen, sitting at the table while my sister put on a fresh pot of coffee. I hadn't seen her in thirty-two long years, and it was jarring to see how she'd aged. I knew my sister colored her hair to hide her grey hair, but I could see fine wrinkles around my sister's eyes and mouth. She was no longer the twenty-two year old girl I'd last seen.

I wondered how much she'd aged since her mate died last year. I felt a stab of guilt that I hadn't been here for her when it happened. No one had told me about it until about a month after he'd passed. I just happened to call my sister and hear the news. I'd asked then if I should come, but Connie had been adamant that she wanted to be alone to grieve. She'd been devastated and depressed, and I was a crappy sister for not insisting on being here for her back then.

I knew her son Drew had moved back to Greysden a few months ago to be closer to her. He'd also found his mate here, which had gone a long way towards helping my sister pull out of her depression at losing her own mate. It was pretty common for lifelong fated mates to die within days of each other, and I was immensely grateful that Connie had been strong enough to survive the loss.

I took a long, bracing sip of the strong coffee. "How's Dad?" I asked.

My sister's eyes filled up with tears. "Gone. You were already on the road, so I figured I would tell you when you got here."

I wasn't surprised. There was no way he was going to go on without her. Our father was dependent on my mother for everything. Well, co-dependent, as my therapist explained to me years ago. As much of an asshole as he was to me, he'd always treated my mom like a queen. Their love was so all-consuming, and they'd been so focused on each other that there had never been anything left for me and my sister. Connie had made her peace with that, but I'd struggled. Still did, if I was being totally honest.

"I'm sorry Connie. I'm sorry I stayed away so long. I'm sorry I wasn't there for you when you needed me."

My sister waved her hand, her face softening with forgiveness and love.

"I understand why you did Angie. After everything that happened with Dad and then losing your mate too…I understand how you felt even better now than I did before. But I always knew that when I really needed you, you would come. And you did. In retrospect, I should have asked you to come when Andy died, but I was so depressed, it was all I could do to hold on. I wasn't thinking clearly. But you're here now, and that's what's important."

I shifted into business mode. "What do we need to do?"

We spent the afternoon making funeral arrangements. Our parents, like most shifters, wanted to be cremated and to have their ashes returned to the woods. We planned a small memorial service at the funeral home, after which the family would disperse the ashes. We were mentally and physically exhausted by the time we got back to Connie's house.

Grabbing two cold beers, we collapsed on the deck in her backyard to relax.

"Gina and Drew want to know if we want to come over for dinner tonight," my sister said, glancing at her phone. "They're looking forward to meeting you."

I felt a stab of guilt that I'd never met my nephew. "Sure, that sounds great."

We rested for a little while, then went back into the house to shower and change clothes. My nephew and his mate lived right next door to my sister, so it wasn't like we needed to go far to get to dinner. As we walked out of the house, Connie nodded at the moving truck parked in the driveway of the house on the other side of hers.

"Oh, it looks like my new neighbor is moving in." She looked over curiously, trying to get a glimpse at what was happening.

Suddenly a loud, deep growl pierced the air. My wolf woke up and started racing around in circles inside me as the hair on the back of my neck rose. I froze in place as I heard a possessive voice growl, "Mine!"

Based on my wolf's reaction, I knew without a doubt they were talking about me.

Damon

I stalked around the truck, looking for my mate. It had been over thirty years, thirty-two in fact, yet I still recognized the sweet scent of oranges and something spicy that was unique to Angie.

My wolf was pushing at my skin, desperate to get out and finally claim our mate. He blamed me for letting her get away all those years ago, and he didn't want to take the risk that I'd fuck it up again.

Hold on there, buddy, I cautioned. *We don't know if she's single or why she's here or what's going on. Let me talk to her first.*

As I cleared the truck I saw her. Angie. My mate. She was older and softer and more rounded than the last time I saw her, but I would recognize her anywhere.

She was about three inches shorter than me, around five foot eight, with lush curves. Large round breasts, an indented waist, rounded hips, thick thighs...even wearing faded jeans and a comfortable short-sleeved knit top she was a vision. She was even sexier than I remembered. Her skin had an olive hue that hinted at her Italian heritage and her dark hair fell to the top of her shoulders in a bob, strands of silver mixed in with the darker hair. But it was her eyes that caught my attention. Brown and deep and looking at me like she couldn't decide if I was the best thing she'd seen today, or the worst.

Her face hardened and I had my answer. I suspected that she'd never forgiven me for not waiting for her, for getting into a relationship with a human instead. I'd never forgiven myself for that either.

I recognized the woman next to her as her sister Connie. I knew that she lived next door to my new house, and while I hadn't seen Connie in years, time had been good to her. She looked great for her age, despite the trauma of losing her mate.

"Connie. Angie. Hello."

Connie gave me a delighted smile. I walked over to her and pulled her into a hug.

"I'm so sorry about Andy," I whispered into her hair. "I didn't know. I just heard the other day."

My realtor had gone to school with all of us and had shared the news that Andy had passed last year. We'd lost touch many years ago and the news never made it to me in Denver. I'd already been planning to come over and pay my respects to Connie once I finished moving in.

As we hugged I heard a soft growl. I looked over and saw that Angie was staring at us like she wanted to rip us both apart. No doubt her wolf was unhappy about me having my arms around her sister. Honestly, mine wasn't thrilled about it either.

Connie pulled away, shooting her sister a speculative look. "Wow, Damon, it's been forever. You look great. I had no idea you were moving back to town."

My wolf was begging me to take Angie into my arms and haul her over to our new den to make her mine, but I shoved him down, admonishing him to be patient. With her arms crossed over her torso and the cold glare she was sending my way, I had the feeling Angie wasn't going to be receptive to getting a hug of her own right now.

"Yeah, I'm semi-retired now, and my kids are all grown with families of their own." I turned to meet Angie's eyes. "Something was calling me to come back home to Greysden."

"And is your wife with you?" Angie asked. The word 'wife' sounded bitter in her mouth.

I shook my head. "She passed away. Ten years ago now."

I saw a flash of relief in Angie's eyes before she shuttered her expression again.

"What about you Angie, are you living here now too?" I hoped so.

She shook her head. "I'm just here for a few days for my parents' funeral, then I'm going back home."

I looked between the sisters. "Oh no, I hadn't heard about your parents. What happened?"

"Mom had a heart attack," Connie explained. "Dad lasted less than twenty-four hours after that. They were always very...close."

"Some would call it co-dependent to the exclusion of others," Angie said bitterly. "We should go Connie, Drew and Gina will be waiting for us."

My heart pinched as she turned away from me.

"We'll talk to you soon Damon," Connie told me, sending me a small smile. "I'd love to catch up with you. Welcome to the neighborhood."

They turned away and walked towards the house on the other side of Connie's. As I watched them walk away, I knew that I'd been right to follow my instincts. I was back in Greysden for a reason, and that reason was right next door. After thirty-some years, I was ready to claim my mate. I just hoped she was willing to be claimed. I knew it wasn't going to be easy, but I wasn't a wolf who backed away from a challenge.

Angie

"Wow, that's a weird coincidence." I could feel my sister's astute gaze on me but pretended like I didn't notice.

Damon Schmitt. What were the chances that I'd run into him here? Last I'd heard he was living in Denver. The minute our eyes met, the years had fallen away like they'd never happened.

He was still impossibly handsome. His body was a little softer than he'd been when we were younger, but he still had a muscled physique and trim waist. One of the best things about being a shifter is that we weren't prone to the same middle-aged spread that humans dealt with. I could still see signs of aging though. Damon's dark blonde hair had faded, his temples almost completely white, and I could see the gray in the scruff that covered his square jaw.

I knew my sister was dying to talk about running into Damon, but thankfully her son Drew answered the door and ushered us into the house as soon as we knocked. I was glad for the distraction. I needed some time to process my feelings about running into my mate and learning that he was no longer married.

I turned my attention to the man who opened the door. My nephew was tall and handsome and looked so much like his father it made my heart squeeze.

"Aunt Angie," he said warmly as he pulled me into a hug. "I'm so glad to finally meet you." Drew stepped back and pulled someone up to join us. "This is my mate Gina. Gina, my Aunt Angie."

I shook her hand and laughed. "Please, just Angie is fine. Thanks for inviting me tonight, Gina, Drew."

"Of course. Please, come in," Gina said warmly.

We followed the younger couple into the house. We were a few minutes late and Gina had already set out food on the table. "I cooked tonight, so you don't have to worry about dying of hunger," she said, winking at her mate. "Drew has many skills, but cooking isn't high on the list."

He pulled her into his side and squeezed her until she squealed. "Show some respect for the man of the house, Mate."

Gina rolled her eyes. "Please, we both know who's in charge around here."

We settled in to eat the delicious meal Gina had prepared. While we ate, Gina and Drew told me about how they'd met in kindergarten and been enemies and rivals all through school. It wasn't until Drew moved back into town again a few months ago and run into each other at a business association meeting that they realized they were fated mates. Apparently it had taken them both a while to accept that news. They were an adorable couple, good-naturedly teasing each other but still very obviously in love.

"Speaking of mates returning to town...," Connie started.

"Don't," I warned, sending her a sharp look.

Gina and Drew looked between us. "What? What are we talking about?"

Ignoring my pointed glare, Connie leaned forward to dish. My sister had always loved gossip. She was well-suited for life in this small town where people traded gossip like it was currency.

"Angie just saw her fated mate. He moved into that house on the other side of me."

Gina looked delighted. "Oh, you finally met your mate? That's so exciting."

"I met him a long time ago, actually," I responded, my tone carefully neutral.

"He was the best man in my wedding," Connie added. "Angie was the maid of honor."

Gina's gaze was teasing. "Oh, you hooked up at the wedding?"

I shook my head. "No. He was already married, and his wife was six months pregnant."

"Why would he marry someone who wasn't his mate?" Gina asked. Although many shifters married for companionship, they generally waited until they were older and reasonably sure that they wouldn't find their fated mate.

"She got pregnant by accident," Connie explained. Clearly she knew more about this part of the story than I did, no doubt hearing more about it from her mate Andy.

"She was a human, and her parents were furious that she'd gotten knocked up by a shifter. They felt like it made them look bad, so they put a lot of pressure on them to get married. Damon wanted to do the right thing, so he married her. Based on the few things Andy told me over the years, I don't think it was a particularly happy marriage. But like a lot of couples, they decided to stay together for their kids."

I felt a stab of bitterness and swallowed it down. There was no sense getting upset about something that had happened so long ago. As painful as it had been to give up my mate, I couldn't fault him for his devotion to his child.

"I can't believe he could stay away from his mate, even if he was married to someone else," Drew said. "My God, I could scarcely stand to be more than a few feet away from Gina after I realized we were mates."

"I, um, left town right after your parents' wedding," I explained. "I had some other serious stuff going on at the time and it was...safest for me to leave town. Plus, I didn't want to make things more complicated for either myself or Damon. It was best for everyone involved that I removed myself from the situation."

Connie's gaze was sympathetic. "I don't want to speak ill of the dead, but you should know that your grandfather treated Angie terribly. He tried to sell her to settle some business debts."

"What?!?!" Drew and Gina spoke as one, outrage clear in their tone.

"Connie, don't," I implored. "It was a long time ago."

My sister ignored me. "Your grandfather had gotten a questionable loan when his business was going under. I still don't know if he knew he was borrowing money from the mob, but the fox shifter in charge took a shining to Angie. He promised Dad he would cancel his debt in exchange for his daughter. Dad agreed to give him Angie as his mate."

"I'm so sorry, Angie. This sounds like the plot of a bad novel," Gina observed.

I still remembered the revulsion I'd felt when I came home the day after Connie's wedding to find the mobster in my parents' living room. The cunning look in the fox's eyes as he'd come close to me, sniffing me, telling me he hoped I was a virgin so he could "break me in". Learning that my father wanted to sell me to the fox to settle his debts.

My mother went along with his plan, as if it was no big deal. "You'll learn to love him," she'd told me. "And he'll provide for you."

Meanwhile the fox stood next to her, making lewd gestures with his tongue. That's the day I decided that my parents were dead to me. I told them I needed a couple of days to think about it. Then I packed up my stuff and drove out of town that very night, cutting ties with my parents. I'd never returned to Greysden again. Until today.

A wave of revulsion hit me, making me nauseous at the memory. The feeling of knowing that my parents considered me disposable. The fear I had as I disappeared and tried to make a life for myself far away from home at such a young age. The desolation of knowing my mate belonged to another. It was a dark time in my life, and I wanted to leave it in the past, where it belonged.

"Please, can we not talk about this?" I begged, placing my hand on my stomach in an effort to settle it back down. "It's all in the past. I left and moved on with my life and Dad, well he probably got what he deserved."

I'd learned years later that the fox had beat Dad up pretty bad after I left. He also seized Dad's business and sold it to someone else to settle the debt. In retrospect, Dad was lucky that he hadn't been killed or worse.

My sister changed the subject, and I tried my best to enjoy the rest of our dinner as the kids told us more stories about Drew's law practice and the designer clothing store Gina ran downtown. By the time I settled into the guest room at Connie's house that night, I'd almost forgotten that my mate was living next door.

Liar, my wolf goaded me.

Damon

I tossed and turned in my bed, unable to sleep. It was my first night in my new house, but I couldn't relax knowing that my mate was right next door. My wolf was scratching at me, whining for me to go find her. I felt the strangest combination of fear and anticipation. Anticipation that I finally could have my shot with my mate, and fear that I would mess it up again and lose her forever.

I heard the sound of a door in the distance and padded over to the bedroom window. Looking down into the neighbor's yard, I saw Angie step out onto the deck, a shadow in the moonlight. Apparently I wasn't the only person who couldn't sleep.

Heading downstairs, I slipped out of my back door and pulled myself over the five foot fence that separated our properties. My mate sat on the deck, eyes trained on me as if she'd known I was coming. And maybe she did. It was inevitable that with us being in such close proximity that our wolves would be encouraging us to spend time together.

"Hey," I called softly. "Can I join you?"

I sensed her hesitation, but she finally nodded. "Okay."

I moved up to the deck and sat beside her on the glider. We rocked for a few minutes, staring at the starry sky, and not talking. Sitting this close to her, I felt a sense of peace that I hadn't felt in years.

"How have you been?" I finally asked.

She turned to look at me. "Are we really doing this?" she asked. "Making small talk?"

"I've been having dreams about you," I shared. "Every night."

"What?" Her brow wrinkled in confusion at my change in topic. I'd forgotten the way she got that little line between her brows when she scrunched up her face. It was adorable.

"The last few months I've been having these vivid dreams that we found each other again. Every night I had the same dream: that we were together here. It's why I moved back to Greysden after being away for all these years. In case my dreams were premonitions."

"You moved across the state because you thought I might show up in Greysden someday?" she asked incredulously. "I haven't been here since the day after Connie's wedding," she told me. "That was a hell of a longshot."

"But you did show up, and on my very first day here too."

"I'm only here long enough to help Connie with my parents' estate, then I'm going back home."

"Where is home these days?" I asked her curiously, ignoring the pinch in my chest at her wanting to leave.

"I live in Washington, just outside of Seattle."

"Did you ever get married?" She wasn't wearing a ring, but that didn't necessarily mean anything.

She shook her head, her expression wry. "There was no way my wolf was going to allow that. She's always been incredibly prickly and hostile around other men. She's hated them all and didn't want me to get near anyone else."

My eyes widened in shock. "So you're still a...?"

Angie laughed, the sound loud in the still of the night.

"Are you seriously asking me if I'm still a virgin? I'm fifty years old for crying out loud. Of course I'm not a virgin. How pathetic do you think I am? Jeez, it's been so long since I got my cherry popped that I don't even remember being a virgin."

My wolf grumbled inside me as she continued to laugh. He was furious that other men had touched our mate. Me reminding him that we'd slept with other women didn't appease him, since he'd never liked that too much either.

"I'm just relieved that you're single," I told her honestly.

"I didn't say that," she rushed to correct me. "I have a boyfriend back home." Her nose wrinkled a little, letting me know that she wasn't too into him. Thank God.

"I tried to find you once. Years ago, after my wife died. I couldn't find you on social media."

"I hate social media," she responded. "I avoid it like the plague."

"I wasn't sure what else to do to find you."

That was a cop-out, and I knew it. I could have asked her sister, I could have hired a private investigator, I could have done more. But instead, I'd continued my self-imposed punishment, living in misery and waiting for fate to send me a sign.

Angie's expression turned sad. "I'm glad you didn't find me, Damon. We were clearly not meant to be."

"My wolf disagrees. And I'm betting yours does too."

"Don't act like you know me," she protested. "We spent a sum total of two days together, over thirty years ago. You have no idea who I am or what I'm thinking, me or my wolf. I'd better get to bed."

She started to stand, but I pulled her back down and positioned her to sit over my lap. She squeaked in protest but didn't fight me.

"What the hell are you doing?" she whisper shouted, wiggling on my lap.

The motion made my cock thicken against my sleep pants, and I clamped one hand down tight on her hip to still her before I started rutting into her like a young pup. The minute she turned her head to glare at me, I wrapped my other hand around the back of her neck, gently compelling her to lower her head.

I pressed my lips against hers, going still as I savored the incredible feeling of having my mate back in my arms again. Her lips were soft and smooth. This close, I could smell the orange spice scent that was uniquely Angie.

We'd kissed once, only once, all those years ago. We'd run into each other in the garden outside the wedding reception and before we could talk, we'd thrown ourselves at each other, passionately kissing. It was the single best kiss of my life. I'd held onto the precious memory of that kiss all these years, keeping it close to me like a kid with a stuffed animal, reliving it over and over again in my mind.

I licked along the seam of Angie's lips, and when she opened with a sigh my tongue swooped in, eager to explore the heat of her mouth. She relaxed into the kiss, her tongue tangling with mine, and we kissed for several long minutes, like teenagers necking in the back of a movie theater.

Angie shifted, moving to straddle me, and I pressed my rock hard cock against her center as she rolled her hips against me. The sleep shirt she was wearing rode high on her legs, and despite the fact that we were outside, I could smell the sweet scent of her arousal.

When Angie finally pulled back, I felt like I'd been hit by a truck. Judging by her expression, she felt the same. Her chest rose rapidly as she tried to control her breath. With my enhanced wolf hearing, I could hear her heart thundering in her chest.

"Damn humans," she whispered.

"What?" I asked in confusion.

"I've only dated humans. Only been with humans," she explained. "I've consciously avoided shifters and now I remember why. Shifters are so primal, they can make you ready to orgasm with only a kiss."

My wolf preened inside me, thrilled that we had satisfied our mate.

"Not just any shifters," I disagreed. "It's that way because we're mates."

She stiffened at the reminder. "We *were* mates," she corrected. "We had our chance, and it's long gone. We're not kids anymore, and I no longer believe in fairy tales."

"Are you telling me you don't feel the connection between us?" I asked. "The sense of rightness now that we're together. Because I think that you do feel it, as much as I do."

She didn't answer. Instead, she slid off my lap and straightened the night shirt she was wearing. My wolf was going insane as she pulled away from us. I tried to convince him that it was okay for her to make a strategic retreat. We had many years of hurt to unravel before we could be together.

"How long are you in town for?" I asked.

Her eyes narrowed at the apparent change in topic. "I took the rest of this week and next off work so I could help Connie," she responded. "I'll head home next weekend, if not sooner."

I stood up, crowding close to her again. Her muscles stiffened, like she was resisting the urge to back away from me.

"I guess that gives me a week then."

"A week for what?" she asked in confusion.

"A week to convince you that this is our second chance. Fate brought us back together again Angie, and there's no way I'm going to let you get away again."

"Damon…"

I held up my hand. "Mark my words, Mate, before the end of the week I'm going to claim you."

"You're crazy," she protested. "We're too old for all this mating crap."

I stared into her eyes, letting her see the glow of my wolf until she shivered. "I've waited a lifetime for you, and I refuse to wait any longer now that I've found you again. You will be mine, Mate."

She was still staring at me with her mouth open when I hopped the fence and returned to my house.

Angie

I was admittedly grumpy when I trudged down to Connie's kitchen the next morning. I'd spent the entire night tossing and turning. Being here, being back in Greysden, was bringing up a lot of memories and emotions that I thought I'd successfully repressed. My mind was filled with memories of my parents, memories of my mate, and a non-stop replay of that kiss with Damon last night.

We'd kissed once before, the night of my sister's wedding. In fact, we'd come close to doing more. It was only the sound of his wife calling out for him in the garden that had brought us back to our senses.

When I'd first seen Damon at the rehearsal dinner my wolf had bounded around ecstatically. Our eyes met and I could tell that he knew, the same as I did, that we were fated mates. Then I glanced down at his left hand and saw the ring. I learned that he'd gotten some human woman pregnant and married her out of a sense of obligation.

We tried to stay away from each other for the wedding weekend, but when we ended up in the garden together, things had gotten a little out of hand and we'd shared a single heart-stopping kiss. Then we'd heard his wife calling for him.

I would never forget the expression on Damon's face as he tried to make a decision between his commitment to the woman he'd just married, and his fated mate. In the end, I'd made it easy for him, pushing him away. I'd told him he needed to stay with his wife and refused to talk to him for the rest of the reception.

I wouldn't be that woman who broke up a marriage, and I knew that once the heat of the moment had passed, Damon would remember that he felt the same. I regretted to this day that I'd let my emotions take over and allowed myself to kiss another woman's husband. It didn't matter that theirs was not a love match. It was still wrong.

"Hard night?" Connie asked wryly as I plopped down at the kitchen table with the largest cup of coffee I could find.

"Couldn't sleep," I grumbled.

"Did it have something to do with a certain wolf shifter I saw vaulting over my fence last night?"

My head popped up so quickly I almost gave myself whiplash. "Um. He was just coming over to say hi."

My sister laughed. "You're a grown woman Angie, you don't owe me any explanations." She leaned forward. "But I would love to hear what happened if you want to share. Once upon a time you were my best friend, and we shared everything."

I took a long sip of coffee, inhaling the delicious scent of the high-end beans my sister used and squashing down the sense of guilt her words brought up in me.

"He said he tried to find me. After his wife died. I guess he looked on social media."

"I wonder why he didn't ask Andy," she mused. "Or hire someone to find you."

I shrugged. "Maybe he thought you guys would protect my privacy. Or maybe he didn't want to find me as much as he told himself he did."

"I was surprised to see he'd moved back here after all this time," Connie remarked.

"He says he's been having these dreams lately. He dreamt of being with me in Greysden, so he decided to move here in case the dreams were prophetic."

"I guess they were, since he found you his very first day back home."

I sent her a pointed look. "Seattle is my home," I reminded her. "Greysden is just the place where I grew up."

"Are you really going to throw away a chance to finally be with your mate?" she asked. "My God, if I could have more time with Andy..." Her eyes filled with tears, but she blinked them away. "Besides, what do you have keeping you in Seattle anyway?"

"Um, my home. My job. My friends. My boyfriend."

"This is the first time you've even mentioned a boyfriend," she said. "Clearly you're not that into him since he didn't come with you. Who is his guy anyway?"

"His name is James. It's not that serious, not enough to bring him here. Besides, he's a human. He doesn't know I'm a shifter."

Many humans knew about the existence of shifters, especially in areas like Greysden where their numbers were numerous. But most of them were blissfully unaware that they were living side by side with people who could turn into animals. Everyone liked it better when shifter stayed off the radar.

"Like I said, you're not that into him."

"I was with him the night you called me," I protested.

Connie gave me her patented 'big sister stare'. I hadn't seen it in thirty years, but it was still effective.

"Fine, you're right. I'm not that into him. We're really better as friends. Also, he sucks in bed. It takes him hours to come. It's super boring."

Connie spewed the coffee that she'd just sipped all over the table. I got up to get a paper towel while she coughed.

When she caught her breath again she asked, "But you come too, right?"

I shook my head. "No, I have to finish myself off with my vibrator after I kick him out. If I'm not too chafed from all that useless pumping anyway."

Connie laughed again, this time without the spray of coffee, fortunately.

"How was it when you kissed Damon last night?"

I looked at her in surprise. "How did you know I kissed him?"

"I didn't," she said smugly. "But now that you told me, how was it?"

I slid down in my chair. "It was incredible, damn it."

"I knew it!" my sister crowed triumphantly. "This is going to be fun."

"What?"

"Watching you finally fall in love with your mate."

Damon

I woke up the next morning feeling better than I had in years. My mate was near, and I had an entire week to convince her to be mine. That was like a century in shifter time. I couldn't wait to finally claim what was mine.

Then get to it, my wolf encouraged. *Don't let our mate get away a second time.*

After taking my wolf out for a long run to check out the woods near my house, I spent the morning unpacking and organizing. I'd gotten rid of a lot of the stuff in my house, and I was glad I'd downsized as I emptied boxes and looked for places to put things away. While I worked, I debated my next steps with my mate.

As it happened, I had an assist. My phone rang in the early afternoon with a call from Connie.

"Hey Damon, it's Connie. I was wondering if you wanted to come over for dinner tonight," she asked. "It's been so nice outside I thought I'd do a barbeque on the deck. My son and his mate will be there too. We scattered my parents' ashes this morning and we're all a little raw. A barbeque will make us all feel better."

"I'd love to, but does your sister know?"

"She will when you get here. See you at six."

Drew and his mate were walking up to Connie's porch the same time as I was. Drew gave me a smile, reaching out to shake my hand.

"Damon, it's been years! It's nice to see you." He pointed at the beautiful woman next to him. "This is my mate Gina. Gina, this is Damon, he was a friend of my dad's. Best man at the wedding."

"Nice to meet you Damon," the younger woman said, giving me a friendly wave of her hand. "We've heard so much about you."

Drew rang the bell and a few seconds later Angie came to open the door. When she looked past Drew and Gina to see me, her face flushed. I noticed the pulse in her throat pick up, telling me that she was as excited to see me as I was to see her.

I grabbed her hand, pulling her outside. "Angie, I'd like a word please."

Drew and Gina gave me sly looks as they headed into the house and closed the door. Angie tugged on her hand, but I held on tight.

"What do you want, Damon?"

"This."

I pressed her against the door and lowered my head, capturing her lips with mine. The kiss was immediately hot, our tongues tangling with each other, hands exploring each other's torsos. When I finally pulled away so we could take a breath, Angie's lips were swollen and red and she looked a little bit dazed. She shook her head, visibly getting her bearings. I could see her re-erecting her emotional barriers.

"We should go in, Connie might need my help with dinner."

"This isn't over, Angie," I promised.

"We can't do this again," she growled, moving her hand between us.

"I think we can."

A glare over her shoulder was her only answer.

I enjoyed a lovely evening with Angie and her family. It was blatantly obvious that her family was invested in getting us together. Connie, Drew, and Gina repeatedly brought the conversation back to myself and Angie, asking questions, talking both of us up, and pointing out all the things we had in common.

I made an effort to be right next to my mate at all times. Maybe I was getting into her space a bit, but as the night went on, I could see her pulse fluttering and her nipples hardening through her shirt with every "accidental" brush of my leg or hand against hers. I only had a week to wear her down, and I wasn't going to waste the opportunity.

"Angie, can you and Damon rinse the dishes and load the dishwasher please?" Connie asked. "I need to go see something at Drew's house."

"You do?" Drew asked in confusion. His mother and his mate both gave him stern looks, and understanding dawned. "Oh yeah, I need to show you the, uh, new washing machine. It's very white."

Angie rolled her eyes at their obvious ploy but didn't call them on their fabrication. After they left, the two of us worked together in silence, with Angie rinsing the dishes and me loading them into the machine. When we finished, I closed the dishwasher and stepped closer to Angie. She must have read the expression on my face because she took a step back, her eyes going wide.

"What are you doing?" she asked.

I took another step forward, and she took another step back, backing herself into the corner where two sides of the counter met. I put one hand on the counter on either side of her, boxing her in, surrounding her but not touching her. Holding her gaze, I lowered my head down to hers, moving slowly. She licked her lips, and I felt my cock twitch in my pants.

"I have been dying to get another taste of you all night," I whispered, a few scant inches away from her lips.

"This is my sister's house," she protested weakly.

"She seems as invested in us getting together as I am," I noted.

"This can't happen," she whispered, even as she swayed nearer. "I'm going home in a few days."

I waited, wanting her, no needing her, to make a move. To show me that this wasn't all in my imagination, that I wasn't the only one desperate to finally claim my mate. Her eyes closed as she swayed forward, her lips touching mine. She kissed me softly and then I took over, tunneling my fingers into her thick hair and deepening the kiss. Angie moaned against my mouth.

My hands moved down and slid beneath her shirt, cupping her breasts with my hands. They were more than a handful, and I couldn't wait to see them unencumbered by her bra. I squeezed her tits, and it was like I'd pressed an 'on' button or something. Suddenly her hands were everywhere, pulling my shirt out of my waistband, fingernails scratching up and down by back.

I broke apart, gasping for breath, and turned her around to face the counter. I pressed between her shoulder blades and Angie lowered her chest onto the counter, her hands gripping the edge. Reaching around to unzip her jeans, I shoved them to her ankles. Her ass was full and round in the satin panties she wore. I unsheathed a claw and ripped them right off her body.

"Hey!" Angie protested.

Her protest died on her lips as my fingers reached around and found her clit. I circled the bundle of nerves a few times before sliding my fingers into her dripping folds. Picking up some of her moisture, I returned my attention to her clit. Meanwhile, using my other hand, I slid two fingers into her opening. I circled her clit and pumped my fingers in and out several times while Angie pushed her hips back against me, trying to encourage me to go deeper.

"Damon, oh my God," she gasped. "Please."

She didn't have to ask me twice. I unzipped my pants, shoving them to my ankles along with my underwear. Without another word, I lined my cock up with her opening and plunged in with one long stroke. Angie made a sound that was halfway between a scream and a moan as the force of my thrust lifted her up on her toes.

I paused, allowing her some time to adjust, nibbling along her neck while I waited.

"You feel so good," she told me. "Now move, damn it."

She didn't need to ask me twice. I started moving slowly, then picked up speed. Angie shoved her hips back, meeting me stroke for stroke.

"Harder," she gasped. "Please. Harder, Damon."

I lowered myself over her back, trapping her against the surface of the counter, and pumped into her like a man possessed. I knew I was probably smashing her into the edge of the counter, but Angie didn't complain. I felt her internal muscles trembling and I knew she was close.

Sliding my hand between her hips and the cabinet, I pinched her clit between my fingers and lowered my head to nip at her ear.

"Come for me, Mate."

She stiffened beneath me, then her entire body started shaking with the force of her orgasm. Her mouth opened with a silent scream. I was a few seconds behind her, groaning out a litany of swear words as I pumped my hips a few more times and released my seed deep in her womb.

"Mine!" I roared. "Mine!"

Angie's pussy pulsed against my cock in response. My wolf was pushing at me to mark her, to make my claiming official, but I held him back. I didn't want to officially make Angie my mate until she was ready. I would not mark her without her consent. I knew instinctively that if I pushed her too hard, too fast, she would run.

When I was done coming harder than I had in my life, I collapsed against her and we lay there on the counter, still joined together and panting, for several long moments. I could feel the exact moment when Angie came out of her post-coital haze. She leveraged her hands against the edge of the counter, pushing us both up to standing, and turned away, disconnecting our bodies.

"Oh my God, I can't believe I just let you fuck me on my sister's counter," she mumbled as she pulled her jeans up. Finding the tattered remains of her panties on the floor, she shoved them in her pocket as she paced back and forth. "I mean, who does that? We're not kids."

After pulling my own pants up, I placed my hands on her shoulders, stalling her motion. She glared at me, all traces of her earlier passion hidden behind her walls again.

"First of all, we're mates, not some random strangers at a frat party," I reminded her. "Second of all, these are mine." I plucked her shredded panties out of her pocket and slid them into mine. "Third of all, that was the single hottest sexual experience I've had in my life. I want nothing more than to do that again and again, every day for the rest of our lives."

Angie's eyes betrayed her inner turmoil. I leaned down and pressed a soft kiss against her lips. "I know you need time, Mate, so I'll go. Unless you want to come home with me tonight?"

She shook her head, and I squeezed her shoulders lightly and pressed my lips gently against her forehead. "Okay then Mate, I'll see you tomorrow."

Angie

I was still standing in the exact same place a full five minutes after Damon left the kitchen. I couldn't believe what had just happened. What was wrong with me? One minute we were loading the dishwasher, and the next thing I knew the man was pocketing the remains of my panties.

Oh my God. It figured that the first non-machine orgasm I'd had in years was with Damon.

He is our mate, he knows how to please us the best, my wolf crowed happily. She was annoyed that Damon and I hadn't marked each other. I'd ignored her increasingly frantic demands to mark Damon while we had sex, as if I could have bit him properly sandwiched between him and the counter. *Your claws were free,* my wolf reminded me petulantly. *You could have scratched your mark on him.*

I rolled my eyes. I knew she was going to be insufferable now. My wolf did not understand why I wasn't overjoyed to be reunited with Damon after all these years. As I lay in bed that night, I asked myself the same question. Why wasn't I overjoyed to find out that Damon and I were both in the same place?

I thought back to my younger self, how devastated I'd been when I realized that my mate was already taken. I knew it was unfair, but I was angry that he hadn't waited for me. Him screwing around with some human had ruined both of our lives. My wolf had wanted to slit the other woman's throat with our claws for daring to touch our mate. She was a jealous little thing who didn't understand that we couldn't hold Damon – or his human wife – responsible for their actions before we even met.

The loss of my mate was all tied up with my feelings about being betrayed by my parents. I'd had nightmares for years where that slimy fox mobster found me and showed me what he meant by breaking me in. Losing my mate and my family all within a twenty-four hour period had been an enormous trauma for me. Even now, I was struggling to separate it.

It was so long ago, and I'd had years of therapy with a very skilled shifter-friendly therapist, so I thought I was over everything that had happened. But being here with my sister, going through my parents' belongings in my childhood home, and finding my mate again after all these years, it was too much. My head was spinning. I hadn't felt this unmoored since the day I'd left Greysden, and I didn't like this feeling. Not one bit.

I liked to feel in control. Safe. I needed it. I didn't like feeling off-kilter like this.

To my surprise, I fell into a deep sleep almost the minute my head hit the pillow. Apparently my kitchen escapades had worn me out. I had to admit that none of my human lovers had given me as much pleasure as Damon had.

When I came downstairs the next morning, I wasn't surprised to see Damon sitting at the table, having coffee with my sister. My wolf grumbled about her being alone with our mate, until I reminded her that Connie had her own mate that she was still mourning.

"Good morning, Sis. Damon stopped by to see you," she said, unnecessarily pointing at him, like I couldn't see the man sitting there as big as life at the kitchen table. "We didn't want to wake you."

"Hey," I said, striving to keep my tone neutral.

"I thought we could take our wolves out for a run today," Damon said.

Despite the elation my wolf felt at the idea, I demurred. "I need to help Connie today, sorry. We're cleaning out our parents' house so we can get it on the market."

Connie bugged her eyes out at me, the way we used to do when we were kids and we wanted to have a silent conversation with each other.

"It's Saturday, and Drew and Gina promised to help," Connie told me. "You go have fun with your mate. We can do without you for one day."

I was torn. I didn't appreciate her shoving us together, but on the other hand, I did appreciate it. Yes, I know, my thoughts were completely contradictory.

Drew walked over to where I stood by the coffee pot, wrapping his arms around me, and pressing his front to my back. He rubbed his cheek against mine, marking me with his scent. My wolf chuffed happily.

"Please come, Angie," he whispered in my ear. "I want to spend the day with you."

I leaned into his embrace, taking a second to enjoy the feeling of being close to him while ignoring my sister's interest in what was happening. All of the sudden her eyes widened. "Oh my God, you had sex in my kitchen last night!"

"What? No! Why would you say that?" I yelped, pulling away from Damon like I'd been burned. "You're being ridiculous."

My sister pointed at me triumphantly. "I *knew* I smelled sex when I came home. It was really concentrated by the side of the sink. I thought it was just my overactive imagination, what with how adamant you've been about not accepting the mating, but now I can see that you two dirty birds got it on last night. Good for you!"

I'd never seen someone so happy that someone else had sex before. I poured myself a cup of coffee while my sister continued chattering, and slid into the chair that was farthest away from where Damon had been sitting. Of course, he immediately moved closer to me. I sighed.

"Are you done?" I asked my sister.

"For now." Her eyes were sparkling with excitement for the first time since I'd gotten here.

"I'm sorry Connie, that was super disrespectful of us to, um, sully your kitchen."

She waved a dismissive hand. "Please, it's not like this kitchen didn't get sullied a time or ten while Andy was still alive. As long as you wiped down the counters afterwards, I'm good."

I shook my head in amusement. I'd forgotten how crazy my sister was. I resolved to talk to her more often when I got back to Seattle. *Maybe I should invite her to come stay with me in Seattle for a while*, I thought.

Suddenly I hunched over in pain as my wolf angrily slashed at my insides. *We are not leaving our mate! No more city. No more humans in our bed. No more rainy weather.*

I resisted reminding my wolf that it also rained a fair amount in Colorado. I realized that my sister and Damon were both watching me, as if they knew that I was fighting with my wolf.

"What do you say, Mate. Are you up for a nice run in the woods? It's a beautiful day."

I met his gaze and caught my breath. God help me, I liked this guy. I liked him a lot. And my wolf wasn't the only one who wanted to spend more time with him. I wanted to learn more about him, get to know him better. I wouldn't mind a repeat of last night either. Just the fact that I'd come on his cock without a bunch of foreplay and the generous use of lube showed me how much I wanted him.

Oh crap, I came on his cock and he'd been bareback. Thank the gods I was in menopause, I hadn't even considered birth control last night.

"Okay," I gave into what I really wanted: to spend time with Damon. I could take the memories back to Seattle with me. "But you'd better buy me brunch afterwards. I'm always starving after a shift."

Damon's handsome face lit up with happiness. "You got it. I'll buy you the biggest brunch you can eat."

Damon

I couldn't believe my luck. I'd thought for sure that Angie would reject my invitation to go for a run. I hoped this meant she was softening towards me. I wasn't completely sure why she was so resistant to the idea of us being mates. Unlike last time we met, neither of us had any obligations that could keep us apart. It felt more like residual anger that I hadn't been available last time we'd found each other.

Whatever our issues were, I was determined to work them out. This second chance was a gift.

We walked a short distance until we got to the woods that ringed the town of Greysden. The town had been founded by grey wolves years ago, but gradually had opened up to other shifters. It didn't matter if you were a wolf, lion, bear, or even a peacock shifter, all were welcome here. Greysden was one of the few shifter-run towns that didn't have an alpha or a hierarchy. It operated just like every other town in America, except most of the residents shared their bodies and souls with animals.

Once we got a little bit farther into the woods, Angie and I both undressed and stashed our clothes beneath a bush. Shifters didn't have the same modesty about being nude around each other, so it felt natural to be naked in front of each other. I watched as Angie took a deep breath and called her wolf forth. A minute later a beautiful greyish brown wolf stood in front of me. She was smaller than my own wolf, but beautiful. Angie's wolf ambled over and rubbed its muzzle against my leg, marking me with her scent. I rubbed between her ears, and she made a sound that was almost like a cat's purr.

She stepped away, looking over her shoulder and encouraging me to follow. I exhaled, feeling the familiar sensation of my body reshaping into its animal form. Once I was shifted, I padded after my mate. We ran through the forest at a leisurely pace, enjoying the warm day. Every once in a while one of us would take a detour, chasing a small animal or sniffing out a particularly interesting smell.

The sunshine was muted by the large trees, but we were still warm by the time we reached a stream deep in the forest. After drinking our fill of the fresh water that came directly from the snowpack in the nearby mountains, we headed back to where we'd left our clothes.

We shifted back to our human forms and retrieved our clothes. Running with my mate had been exhilarating, but I was super hungry after all that exercise.

"Where's the best breakfast in Greysden?" I asked.

She shrugged. "I've been gone as long as you have," she reminded me. "But when I drove through town, I noticed that the Xanakis Diner was still there."

"I used to love that place. Let's go."

We walked hand in hand towards the little "downtown" area of Greysden. It was quirky and slightly old-fashioned. On one side of the Main Street there were rows of shops, on the other were municipal buildings, a large park space where festivals were held, and the same diner I'd eaten at a million times when I was a kid. It felt like coming home when I slid into a cracked red booth across from my mate.

Despite our long absences, several people in the diner recognized one or both of us, including the owner, Mr. Xenakis. The badger shifter greeted us with hugs, like we were long-lost friends. We ordered two breakfast platters, coffee, and orange juice. Angie and I were both starving after our long run, and we ate every crumb of food on our massive plates.

Angie leaned back with a contented sigh.

"That's the nice thing about hanging out with other shifters," she said. "I can eat as much as I want without people looking at me weird."

"What do you mean?" I asked.

"Well, the guy I'm kind of seeing, James? The first time I went out to dinner with him he took me to a Thai restaurant. I'd gotten distracted at work, so I hadn't eaten all day, so you know how that was, my wolf was damn near ripping me open to get some food. I ate a giant bowl of hot and sour soup, an entire platter of phad thai, two eggrolls, and some crab puffs. I looked up and he was just staring at me like I was some kind of freak. Then he made a joke about how I was able to keep my trim figure if I ate like that."

"He doesn't know you're a shifter?" I asked.

Angie shook her head. "I'm not even certain if he knows that shifters exist."

She paused, then said, "I never asked you about the baby you had. Are they a shifter?"

When a shifter mated with a human, there was a fifty/fifty chance of the child getting the shifter gene.

I shook my head. "Both of my daughters are full humans."

I saw a flash of pain in her eyes at the mention of a second child. "And your wife, did she know about your true nature?"

I nodded. "I had to tell her when she got pregnant, just in case. It always freaked her out and after seeing me shift once, she told me to never do it in front of her or the kids again. She told me once that she was glad both of our kids turned out, as she said, normal."

Angie winced. "I'm sorry."

I gave her a smile. "Don't be. My girls are great, even if they are just humans. Amy is thirty-one now, married with three great kids. My youngest, Abby, just turned thirty. She and her husband just had their second baby."

"Wow, five grandkids. Good for you, old man," she teased.

"It's weird being this age," I confided. "In my head, I'm maybe twenty-two. How can I possibly be a grandpa? Then I look in the mirror and think, who is this old guy with the grey hair?"

Angie smiled. "Yeah, one day I was getting ready to leave the house and I looked down and was like, whose old lady hands are these coming out of the sleeve of my jacket?"

"You're still as beautiful as the day I met you," I told her sincerely. "The years have been good to you."

Her cheeks turned pink. "You're not too bad yourself. The truth is, we're both a little older, a little softer, but we're both aging pretty well I think. We've got a lot of years left in us."

"Shifter genes for the win," I laughed. "What do you want to do now?"

She looked embarrassed. "Take a nap? Now that I've exercised and eaten a big meal, I'm super tired."

"I've got just the place."

Angie

I woke up snuggled with Damon in a large hammock that was hanging between two huge fir trees in his backyard. When we'd gotten back to his place, he'd convinced me to snuggle in the hammock with him. To both of our surprise, I'd agreed. There was no funny business, just napping. He'd tucked my head onto his chest, and I could hear his steady heartbeat beneath my ear. It was nice waking up with him, nicer than I would even admit to myself. I shifted a bit, realizing that my foot was falling asleep, and Damon startled awake.

"What time is it?" he asked, his voice raspy.

"No clue, but I really need to pee." That was one of the joys of being in my fifties: I pretty much always needed to pee.

"Let's go inside."

I took care of my business, then wandered around checking out Damon's house. It was a carbon copy of my sister's house next door, except everything was flipped in the other direction. There were boxes lining the walls, all neatly labeled. I found Damon in the living room. Our eyes met, and I was suddenly very very horny. I stalked towards him and put my arms around his neck.

"What do you want to do now?" I asked, making my voice sultry.

Damon's eyes widened. I stepped closer and felt his cock twitch against my belly. I pulled his head down for a kiss. Our tongues dueled for control as the kiss intensified. I rolled my pelvis against him, trying to get closer, and he stepped back, breathing heavily.

"What's the matter?" I asked in confusion. It was clear he wanted me, what with the enormous erection tenting his pants.

"I can't do this," he said. "I can't make love to you again without marking you."

My wolf whined inside me, begging me to agree to complete the mate bond. I shushed her. "There will be no marking," I said firmly.

"No mark, no sex," he said stubbornly.

"You can't be serious."

"I've never been more serious in my life."

I pushed away from him with a huff. "Fine!"

I was incredibly irritated and yet I appreciated him being honest about his feelings. I was dying to get out of here, but I knew my wolf would give me hell if we left things like this.

"Do you want some help with this stuff then?" I asked, waving my hands at the stack of boxes along the wall. If we weren't going to fuck, I needed another outlet to burn off my energy.

"You want to help me unpack?" he asked in surprise.

"I have an ulterior motive. We could use your boxes to pack up my parents' house. Besides, I'm going to need something to distract me."

He smiled, knowing exactly what I wanted to be distracted from. "How about you help me unpack today, and I'll help you and Connie at your parents' house tomorrow?"

"Sounds like a plan."

The next couple of days passed in a blur. We spent the rest of the day unpacking and organizing Damon's house, then moved over to pack up my parents' house. Connie and the kids had separated things out for us, so it was easy to pack up the items no one wanted and drop them off at the charity store. Hopefully someone could use the things that our family didn't want.

Damon was a champ, working just as hard as me and my sister, if not harder, and between the three of us the house was mostly packed up in three days, much faster than I would have expected given the amount of crap my parents had accumulated. The only vexing part was that Damon was treating me like I was his buddy instead of a woman he desired. Despite all my hints, he'd kept me firmly in the friend zone.

The night we finished packing up the house the three of us had dinner at Connie's house. After dinner, Connie begged off with a headache that was clearly fake, leaving us alone. Damon and I hadn't done much more than engage in a few furtive glances and subtle touches since the day we went for a run with our wolves, and I was starting to wonder if his interest in me was waning.

I was obsessed with him in a way I didn't want to admit, and the more time that went by without him touching me, the more keyed up I felt. I'd masturbated more in the last few days than I had in the past few months. My body was on fire every second we were together, and my wolf was driving me crazy, begging me to mark him so everyone would know that Damon was ours.

After Connie went upstairs, Damon and I headed into the backyard. It was a warm beautiful night, and I loved sitting in the fresh air. We sat side by side in the glider where we'd sat the first night we'd gotten there. I was cuddled under his arm, my hand on his thigh.

"Can I ask you something?" he asked.

"Yeah?"

"What's your objection to us being together? We were apart for so long, I don't get why you aren't more excited about us finding each other again. Why don't you want to mate with me?"

"My life is in Seattle now, not here." My answer was lame, and we both knew it.

"What if I moved to Seattle?" he asked.

I stiffened. "You just bought a house here."

"So? My mate is more important than any house."

I bit back a sigh. "Listen Damon, I like you. I like you a lot. You're a great guy. But things just aren't going to work out with us; we had our chance and it passed. It's been too long, and I'm too old and set in my ways to take a mate now. But clearly we are physically compatible, so I'll offer again, if you're up for a short term affair while I'm here, I would love that."

That was an understatement. I yearned to feel his skin against mine at least one more time. Our quickie in the kitchen was by far the best sex I'd had in my life, and there was no way I wanted to turn down more orgasms if they were on the table.

"No."

Or not.

"What do you mean no? I'm offering you a no-strings fling. That's every man's dream."

Part of me knew I was lying to myself though. The truth was, I wanted to spend time with him, and the more time I spent with him, the harder it was to remember my objections to taking a mate.

"We are not having sex again until you admit that you're my mate and we agree to mark each other," he said stubbornly.

"What?" I leapt up and moved away from him, needing my distance. I couldn't decide if I was frustrated, angry, or impressed that he was sticking to his guns. I wasn't one to beg for sex, but if I was, I'd be begging right now.

"I settled for less than I deserved once, Angie, and while I'm grateful that I got my daughters out of that relationship, I would rather be alone than cheapen our relationship with meaningless sex and then have you disappear again."

I threw up my hands. "Oh my God, you're being so unreasonable."

I realized with a start that I was hurt that he'd never come looking for me. Not after his kids were adults, not after his wife died. "If you wanted me so bad, you could have found me before thirty years had passed," I snipped, hearing the hurt in my voice.

Damon got up from the glider and stalked towards me. It took everything in me not to run away from the predatory look in his eyes. When he got close, he gripped my hair in his hand, holding my head still, and meeting my eyes.

"I was an idiot for not finding you sooner, but I'm not going to make that same mistake again."

He lowered his head and kissed me until we were both breathless.

He pulled my head to the side, nipping down the side of my neck before focusing his attention right where my neck and shoulder met. He nipped me hard enough to make me yelp, then kissed away the sting.

"This is where I'm going to mark you," he told me. "When you're ready."

"What if I'm never ready?" I whispered before I could stop myself.

I'd seen what having a mate did for my parents. It had made them co-dependent and so obsessed with each other that they hadn't batted an eye when their loan shark wanted to forcibly mate their daughter. Losing my parents and losing my mate in the same twenty-four hour period had broken me. I could never love again.

Damon looked into my eyes for a long moment. "Someday you'll trust me enough to tell me what's really going on. This isn't only about the decision we made to stay apart all those years ago, or me not finding you sooner. There's something else that's making you think you don't deserve love, or that you can't care for me."

I opened my mouth to protest, and he placed one finger over my lips.

"That's okay Angie, I love you enough for the both of us."

I gasped against his finger.

Love? He was talking about love? We'd been back in each other's lives for only a few days. We weren't pups anymore, filled with dreams of happily ever after.

Damon gave me a sad smile. "Someday soon, you'll realize that you love me too."

Damon

As I walked away from Angie I hoped I was doing the right thing. I needed to convince her that we were meant to be, and that it wasn't too late for us. The way I figured it was that I had two options: to love her up so hard that she wouldn't notice that I marked her until it was too late, or withhold what she wanted – what we both wanted – until she was desperate enough to commit.

My wolf was firmly in the "mark her now" camp, but I wasn't sure. It was a gamble playing it this way, but I knew instinctively that my best shot with my mate was to wait for her to make a conscious choice for us to be together.

I wish I knew what was holding her back. It was more than pique that I hadn't been available all those years ago. She'd made the choice for us. I remembered waffling that night we kissed, torn between my commitment to my wife and the intense desire to be with my fated mate. In the end, Angie had been stronger than I was. She'd walked away, and as much as it killed me, I'd been grateful for it. If I'd abandoned my wife and kids, I would have never been able to forgive myself.

But I'd known then, as sure as I knew my own name, that we'd be together again someday. I'd always accepted that fate would bring us back together again when the time was right. That's why I hadn't searched for her as soon as I could have. Maybe it was yet another mistake I'd made with her, but I was waiting for a sign. That's why when I started having dreams of being with her in Greysden I knew I had to move back here. The sign had come.

That night I'd fucked her in the kitchen hadn't gone as I'd hoped for. I'd always thought when I took my mate for the first time things would be a little more romantic. A candlelight dinner maybe. Definitely a bed. I never imagined that I'd be so overcome with desire for her that I'd lean her over the countertop and rut into her like an animal. Not that she seemed to mind at the time. She clearly wanted more.

The more time I spent with my mate, the stronger the bond between us became, even without us marking each other. I was starting to understand my mate on a level that couldn't be explained by our short relationship. My wolf instincts had told me that Angie could compartmentalize, that she was good at compartmentalizing. She thought if we framed our relationship as a short-term fling we could both walk away.

I knew that wasn't true, but I was still resolved to hold out for a commitment. I wanted to do things the right way this time. Eventually she would break. I was sure of it. In the meantime, I hoped I could figure out what was holding her back.

The next day I stuck to her like glue. Wherever she was, I was right beside her in her space, purposely brushing against her or touching her shoulder or making sure our hands connected when we passed boxes off between us. I'd pretty much had a hard-on all day and judging by the delicious scent of arousal coming off my mate, her panties were soaked.

The minute Connie left to take a load of boxes to the thrift store I pounced. Angie was closing the front door and I moved up behind her, crowding her against the door.

"What are you doing?" she whispered breathlessly.

"Nothing," I said, forcing my voice to sound detached and calm.

I wrapped my hands around her hips, pressing my erection against her ass. I lowered my lips, kissing and nipping along the side of her neck as I slowly ground into her from behind, letting her know just how much she affected me. Angie moaned, turning her cheek to rest against the door. Reaching around, I unsnapped her jeans and shoved them to the top of her thighs, just enough to give me access to her pussy. At the same time, I nudged the neck of her shirt over with my nose so I could grip the muscle along the top of her shoulder in my teeth.

"No biting," she said breathily.

"Wouldn't dream of it," I responded, nipping her there and then trailing tiny little bites across the top of her shoulder.

Meanwhile I dipped my hand down the front of her panties, cupping her mound with my hand. Slowly, so slowly, I slipped my fingers in between her folds. As I expected, she was slick with arousal. I pushed my index finger into her channel and began pumping in and out, keeping the heel of my hand pressed tightly against her clit.

Angie rubbed herself against my hand, seeking more pressure. She moaned as I added a second finger and resumed my assault. I kept my other hand on her hip, holding her in place with just the tips of my claws pressing into her.

"Fuck," she wailed. "Oh my God! That feels so good!"

The minute I felt her internal muscles start to spasm, I pulled my hand away. She tilted her pelvis, trying to follow my fingers, but I stepped back.

"What—-, what's wrong?" she gasped. "I was so close."

"Sorry, no mate mark, no love."

Angie whipped around so fast she almost fell over. Yanking her jeans up, she gave me a glare that could melt steel.

"You know what you are?" she hissed, stalking forward to drill a finger into my chest. "You're a clit tease. I can't believe you!"

I forced myself to shrug nonchalantly instead of throwing her to the floor and finishing what we'd started.

"I've been clear about what I want."

"Fine, if that's the way you want it, this is war!"

As she slammed out of the door with a huff I stifled a laugh. She was hot as hell when she was angry, and I knew without a doubt my plan was going to work.

The next two days I kept up my approach. Wherever Angie was, I was right next to her. I "accidentally" brushed against her at every opportunity. And whenever Connie left the room, I pushed my mate up against the wall and kissed her senseless, then stepped back, leaving her panting and needy.

Meanwhile Angie took any chance she could to tease me back. She wore low-cut shirts and short shorts, displaying a body that was still incredibly fit for someone our age. When we passed each other she managed to brush my cock with her hand or her hip, and kept sending me sultry looks, ensuring that I was half hard whenever she was near.

Angie was becoming increasingly cranky the longer I held out, snapping at both me and her sister when we tried to talk to her. Connie clearly knew something was going on between us, but other than shooting curious looks between us, she didn't comment on our battle of the wills.

We were both in a perpetual state of arousal and after two days of teasing each other, I wondered how long we could keep on before one of us broke. I couldn't wait to find out.

Angie

"What's going on with you and your mate?" Connie asked. "You're giving off so many pheromones even I'm getting horny."

I choked on my coffee. "Oh my gosh, that's TMI, Sis."

My sister gave me a hard look. "Seriously, all those longing looks and secret touches. I'm confused. Are you guys getting together or not?"

"Definitely not."

Connie's eyes darted to the corner of the kitchen where Damon and I had sex several days ago. "But you..."

I rolled my eyes. "It was just the one time, I told him that. I offered a short-term affair, and he declined my offer."

Connie raised one eyebrow and stared me down.

"OK, fine, the truth is we...um, started some stuff a few times but then he...um, stopped before I got to the finish line. He says we're not going to have any sexy times until I agree to finalize the mating, and he's trying to coerce me into it by making me insane with lust."

Connie laughed. "I can't believe your mate is giving you lady blue balls. That's hilarious."

"I'm glad you think so," I grumbled, "because I'm well past the point where my vibrator is getting the job done."

"What's the problem Angie? You didn't want him to leave his wife back then, and you left town anyway so he couldn't have changed his mind about staying with his wife. You're both single now, what's the sense in torturing yourself and each other? Why not go for it?"

I stared at her like she was crazy. "You've seen what having a mate can do, Connie. You saw Mom and Dad be so wrapped up in each other they had no interest in anyone else, including their own daughters. And did you forget the way they freaking tried to hand me over to a slimy mafia dude to pay their debts? They were selfish and co-dependent and if that's what having a mate means, I want no part of it."

Connie's eyes softened. "I know they were a bad example, but you weren't here to see a good example. Andy and I were not like that. He never tried to control me. We both had our own friends and our own careers and our own lives in addition to the life we had together. And Drew, well, our son was always our highest priority. If you ask him he will probably tell you that we paid *too much* attention to him."

She reached across the table to lay her hand over mine. "You know how I made that work? Whenever I had a doubt how to be in a committed relationship with my mate or how to be a good parent, I asked myself, 'what would Mom and Dad do?' and then I did the exact opposite. It worked like a charm."

"You raised a good one," I reassured her. "Drew is awesome."

"And so are you. It breaks my heart to see you throwing away a shot at happiness. I know how hard it's been for you to live without your mate, the same way Andy and I were separated for those four years."

Connie had met Andy a couple of days before she was due to go away for college. Andy had wanted them to mate right away, but in the end he'd accepted her wishes to go away and have some adventures. They'd stayed away from each other for four years, until she had her degree. They'd married soon after she graduated.

"It was terrible, but not as terrible as it was the day I realized that he was dead, and there was no way I could ever see him again."

My sister's eyes filled with tears, but she blinked them away. "My greatest wish for you is to be as happy as I was with Andy. To be as happy as Drew and Gina. Don't let our parents have power over you anymore Angie. Take a chance on being happy."

"I am happy," I answered stubbornly. "I have a good life in Seattle."

"What if you could have a better life here? With Damon?"

We both started as we heard a crash followed by a horn honking. Looking at each other curiously, we headed out to the front porch to see what was going on. Someone had taken out Connie's mailbox. It lay flattened under the front of a car with Washington plates. A car that looked familiar.

"Oh my God Angie, thank God I found you!"

I looked up to see James, my sort-of boyfriend, jump out of the car and rush across the lawn. Connie and I descended the stairs to meet him halfway.

"What did you do to my mailbox?" she called out in irritation.

"Sorry about that, I was looking at my phone to see if I had the right house. I had to ask people in town where you live since Angie wasn't answering my calls. I promise I'll pay for it."

"You bet your ass you will," Connie grumbled as she moved the ruined mailbox out of the street.

Before she could say more James grabbed me and pulled me into a hug. "Angie, baby, I came as soon as I heard what happened."

He pulled away a bit to give me a chastising look that immediately raised my hackles.

"I was worried when you weren't answering my texts. I can't believe I had to hear from your neighbor that you were in Colorado because your mother died. Why didn't you call me? I'm your boyfriend, you know I would have come with you. You didn't need to do this alone."

I opened my mouth to respond that I wasn't alone, but before I could get the words out James lowered his head and kissed me hard. I grabbed onto his shoulders to keep my balance, too shocked at his unexpected appearance to do anything else but hold on.

Notice how you feel nothing when you kiss him, my wolf crowed. *It's nothing like when you kiss our mate.*

My wolf wasn't lying. I thought his kisses were okay before, passable but not the best, but now compared to Damon it felt like I was kissing a dead fish. I immediately chastised myself for my uncharitable thoughts. James was a good guy, even if I wasn't all that attracted to him.

James pulled away long enough to whisper, "I missed you, baby. Why won't you let me get close to you?"

Before I could respond he was kissing me again. I stood still in his embrace, not really kissing him back, but not pulling away either. I heard a deep angry growl that made the hair on the back of my neck stand up. Before I could process what I was hearing, James went flying back through the air, almost taking me with him.

"Get the hell away from my mate!"

I looked down to see James flat on his back on the grass, a pissed off Damon standing over him with his fangs extended. Crap.

I stalked over and pushed Damon out of the way, hissing "Retract your fangs!"

Dropping to my knees, I looked at my kind-of boyfriend. "James, are you all right?"

He sat up with a petulant look, rubbing the back of his head. "Yeah, I think so. What's up with that dude attacking me like that?"

"That 'dude' is her mate, and I don't like your hands on her," Damon growled. "Tell him, Angie."

James pushed to his feet, puffing out his chest and bravely turning to face Damon, even though my mate had a good five inches on him. "That's my girlfriend you're talking about."

"She's mine now."

I stepped between them with a glare.

"I don't belong to anyone," I said firmly. "You can stop the posturing, boys. You both have big dicks. I've seen them both up close. There's no need to pull them out and measure who's the bigger man."

I heard another angry growl. "That's it, I'm done being patient."

Before I could form a response, Damon grabbed me and threw me over his shoulder like a sack of potatoes. I gasped in shock.

"Put me down asshole!" I shouted, pounding on his back.

"Hey, stop manhandling my girlfriend," James yelled at the same time.

"I'm not your girlfriend," I protested at the exact same time Damon snarled, "She's not your girlfriend!"

James gasped in outrage, but seemed frozen on the spot. I almost felt bad for him. I wasn't happy that he'd come here without permission, but I knew he was trying to be a good guy. I was sure he wasn't expecting to see some guy carrying me away on his shoulder like something out of one of those old movies.

"Angie! Where are you going? I just got here!"

"I'm sorry, but this is really not a good time, James," I heard Connie tell him as Damon carried me across the grass to his house. "Angie needs to be with her family right now."

"I drove two days to get here to support her!"

"I'm sorry you came all this way, James, but I didn't ask you to do that," I called, using my claws to try to climb off Damon's shoulder. He laid a firm smack on my ass, making me squeak.

"Angie!" James' voice turned angry, as if he suddenly realized there was a reason I was over some other guy's shoulder. "Have you been cheating on me with this Neanderthal?"

"I'm not your girlfriend," I reminded him again. "I told you repeatedly that we were non-exclusive and were not going to get serious. I'm sorry things went down this way, but it's really best if you go back to Seattle."

I felt bad that James was so upset, and in retrospect I guess I should have responded to his dozens of texts, but I'd told him over and over again from the day we met that I just wanted something casual. But this? Driving across several states to arrive unannounced? I never expected this from him. I thought he understood what we were, what the nature of our relationship was. I reminded myself that it wasn't my fault that he'd ignored my words and decided he could convince me to change my mind.

"I should have known you were stepping out on me with other guys when you refused to let me sleep over," James said nastily. "I can't believe I wasted time coming here to be treated like this. Selfish bitch!"

Damon growled deep in his throat, but I gave him my own warning growl and he kept marching towards his house.

"The freeway is just that way," Connie said helpfully, pointing up the street. "Just head back on Main Street like you did when you came in."

James moved back to his car, ranting and swearing the entire time. "Don't come crawling back to me later Angie. We are through!"

And with a squeal of tires, he was gone.

Damon

I had never once manhandled a woman. Until today. I'd come outside when I heard the crash as that idiot knocked over Connie's mailbox and when I saw him kiss my mate I'd seen red. I had literally never been this angry in my entire fifty-five years. It had taken every ounce of my self-control to hold my wolf back so he wouldn't rip the human's throat out.

Like he deserves for touching our mate, my wolf added.

I stalked into the house with Angie wiggling on my shoulder like a fish on a hook. "Damn it Damon, put me down!"

I ignored her, walking through the house to the master bedroom. Slamming the door behind me, I tossed her on the bed. Angie immediately pushed herself up and stomped towards me.

"What. The. Fuck. Is Wrong. With you?"

She poked me in the chest with every word. I captured her hand in mine. "I can't believe you kissed that ridiculous human."

Her eyes were pure fire. "First of all, he kissed me. Secondly, who I kiss or don't kiss is my business not yours!"

I used my hold on her hand to tug her closer to me.

"That's what you think, little mate."

She smacked me on the chest with her other hand. "Quit calling me that."

I could feel my fangs press against my gums again and tried to calm down. I took a deep breath and lowered my voice.

"I'm not waiting anymore for you to come around, clearly you need a push."

Her eyes widened. "What do you mean?"

I pointed to the bed. "Take off your clothes and get on the bed. I'm doing what I should have done the first time I saw you: I'm activating the mate bond."

Although it was possible to officially mate just with a bite, the process was less painful and much more enjoyable if the partners were in the middle of an orgasm when it happened. It also made the bond strengthen that much quicker.

"Bite me, asshole!"

"That's my plan, baby."

Grabbing her shoulders, I pulled Angie close. Before she could protest, I pressed my lips against hers. I licked along the seam, seeking entrance, but she stood in place, her entire body stiff against me. I nipped her lip and when she yelped in outrage, my tongue slid into her mouth. Our tongues fought for dominance, teeth and lips mashing together.

I could smell the sweet smell of her arousal and I pulled her closer, close enough that we were pressed together from knees to shoulders. I lowered my hands to cup the soft globes of her ass, squeezing her. She retaliated by digging the tips of her claws into my shoulders. I broke away with a yelp. Ripping my shirt over my head, I glanced down to see the marks she'd left. My wolf crowed happily at the idea that she'd marked us.

"Careful sweetheart, you almost broke the skin."

"I'll break your head in about two minutes," she grumbled.

I reached for her shirt, pulling the edges apart. Buttons flew everywhere as she protested. "Hey! I like this shirt."

"I told you to take off your clothes," I reminded her.

"I told you to take off your clothes," she mimicked, her voice deep in an impression of me. "You're just the passive little woman, you must do what I say."

"Well it would be much easier that way," I said mildly.

She smacked me in the chest again. Whatever she was going to say next was lost as I reached down and pinched her nipples through the thin fabric of her bra. They hardened under my fingertips and Angie hissed.

"How do you like it?" she asked, pinching my own nipples. I winced at the bite of pain. My mate was not being gentle with me, and it just ratcheted up my excitement.

"I love it when you're rough, mate."

She stepped back with a small scream. "You're impossible."

I followed her, pulling her close to kiss her again. Our kiss was angry and passionate and enough to have me so hard I was afraid I was going to come in my pants like a teenager.

I backed Angie up until the back of her knees hit the bed. Giving her a gentle shove, I dropped to my knees on the side of the bed and practically tore off her jeans and underwear. Putting her thighs over my shoulders, I leaned down and licked her from bottom to top. She made a keening noise as I did it twice more. She was soaking wet, and my tongue moved easily through her slick folds.

Angie pushed herself up to her elbows to watch me. "I don't like you very much right now," she panted.

"You want me to stop?" I asked, raising one eyebrow.

"God, no."

I felt a thrill of triumph at her acquiescence. Holding her gaze, I slipped one finger into her channel and began pumping in and out. I added a second finger and curled them both in the "come here" motion, touching the rough patch of tissue that was her G-spot. Angie yelped and dropped back down on the bed. I loved how responsive she was to my touch.

Lowering my head again, I began to circle her clit with my tongue while continuing to fuck her with my fingers. I could feel her muscles spasming around my fingers and knew she was close. I glanced up to see that Angie was gripping the bedspread with her claws extended, ripping the fabric as she tossed her head from side to side in ecstasy. I returned to her clit, sucking it into my mouth and gently biting down.

Angie's orgasm hit her hard. She spasmed hard against my fingers and jackknifed off the bed before falling back down with a groan. "Fuuuck!"

I slowed my pace as she came down from her orgasm. I leapt to my feet, shucking my shoes and pants. My cock was angrier than I'd ever seen it, the veins standing at sharp contrast to the red skin. I squeezed the tip and recited baseball stats in my head to calm down a bit. When I felt I was back in control I lowered myself over Angie's prone body and kissed her deeply.

"Oh no," she said, rolling us over so she was on top. "You don't get to be the dominant one. You don't get to be in control."

"Maybe we can take turns," I suggested as I rolled us over again.

Angie bent her knees, digging her feet into the mattress for traction, and turned us again. Unfortunately, we were out of bed space so instead we went crashing to the floor, Angie on top of me. I landed with a grunt. In the second it took for me to catch my breath from the fall, my mate moved over me, straddling my hips, and lining my cock up with her opening.

She looked down at me. "This doesn't mean I'm not still mad at you," she warned.

"Understood."

Angie slid down, taking my hard cock into her heat. We both moaned as our hips connected. She took a few second to adjust, then began moving up and down, riding me with a triumphant smile on her face. Up and down she moved, slowly, so slowly it was driving me crazy. Every time our bodies met she did some kind of a swirly movement with her hips that heightened my pleasure.

My wolf was beside himself, overjoyed at her display of strength. He might be an alpha wolf, but he appreciated that his mate was also an alpha. *Our mate is strong, she takes what she wants,* he noted approvingly.

I was close to coming undone, fighting to keep control. I wanted to make it last. I needed her to come one more time before I joined us forever.

When I saw Angie's fingers creep down to circle her clit, I surged up to a seated position and pulled her hands to my shoulders.

"Mine," I growled, replacing her fingers with my own.

Angie immediately stopped moving. "I'm not yours. I'm not anybody's." Her voice was firm and stubborn.

I was surprised to see a flash of hurt and vulnerability in her eyes instead of the anger I was expecting. I placed one hand on each side of her face, waiting for her to meet my eyes.

"You're my mate Angie. I love you. I've always loved you, and I always will. I'm yours as much as you are mine. I don't want to change you, I like you just the way you are. I don't know what happened to make you so skittish, but I hope you'll tell me some day."

She stared into my eyes as if trying to read the truth of my words. Coming to a decision, she began moving again. Her hands gripped my shoulders for leverage as she bounced up and down on my cock, her heavy breasts dragging against my chest with every movement. My mate wasn't young anymore, but she had a curvy soft body that was every bit as attractive to me as it had been when she was younger and leaner.

I leaned forward and took her earlobe between my teeth, gently nipping her while my hands squeezed her ass. Her mouth opened in a silent scream as she reached her release, and I was right behind her, jerking my hips up as I painted the walls of her womb with my seed.

Without conscious thought, my fangs descended and sunk into the muscle at the top of her shoulder, marking her forever as my mate. The movement triggered another orgasm. I could feel her internal muscles squeezing me so hard I thought I might black out.

To my surprise, I heard Angie growl "mine" and then she was biting my shoulder, marking me with her sharp wolf teeth. My wolf howled happily inside me as the mate bond activated.

We both stopped moving, licking each other's wounds to seal them. I could feel the mate bond pulsing between us. It would grow stronger the more time we spent together, but I could already feel my mate's emotions in a way I hadn't felt an hour ago. Whatever happened next, we were tied together forever now.

Angie lifted her gaze to mine, looking shell-shocked. I could feel a riot of conflicting emotions moving through her: joy, fear, confusion, and lust.

"I can't believe I just did that," she said, almost to herself. "I can't believe I lost control."

"Let's snuggle for a while," I suggested, gently lifting her off me so we could move back to the bed. "We need some time to recover."

Angie

Damon moved to standing and reached out a hand, pulling me to my feet. We didn't say a word as he led me to the bed, pulling the blanket over our naked bodies and dragging me against him. I snuggled into his warm body, laying my head on his shoulder while he wrapped his arm around me. I felt comfortable and safe in his arms, and while I expected that thought to freak me out, for some reason it didn't.

We lay in silence for a few minutes, and I thought maybe Damon had dozed off until he finally spoke.

"Are you okay?"

We were officially mates now that we'd marked each other. Even though I never planned for that to happen, I couldn't say that I was sad about it. Despite my reservations, now that it had happened, it felt right. I could feel his love for me through the mate bond. I knew I needed to tell him about my history, so we could put it behind us.

"My parents were a bad example of being mates," I started.

"Were they fated mates?" he asked. We both knew that shifters oftentimes gave up on finding their fated mates and settled for a regular mate, similar to a human marriage. Some of those relationships worked out well, some did not.

"They were fated mates, and from the minute they laid eyes on each other, everyone else ceased to exist."

"That's how it is with mates."

I shook my head.

"No, you don't understand. They were completely co-dependent. They had a kind of...unhealthy obsession with each other. They were fixated on each other to the exclusion of almost everything else. They had no friends, no outside interests, nothing else mattered to them, not even their kids. Connie and I had to learn early on how to take care of ourselves, because our parents were too oblivious to do more than the bare minimum."

"I remember meeting them at the wedding," he said thoughtfully. "Now that you mention it, I remember thinking it was weird that they were so disinterested in Connie and Andy and the guests. They spent the whole reception alone, avoiding conversation with anyone else."

"Yeah, that's exactly how they were all the time," I explained. "The day after Connie's wedding, after you and I agreed to stay apart, I came home to find this sleazy old fox shifter in the living room with my parents."

He stiffened beneath me, no doubt suspecting from my tone that he wasn't going to like where this was going. I rubbed his chest with one hand, instinctively offering him comfort.

"The fox was a loan shark or with the mafia or something, and my father had taken out a loan from him to bail out his business."

"Your father got mixed up with a loan shark?" he asked in surprise.

"Yeah, he did. When I came into the house, the fox looked me over like I was the prize heifer at the fair. I'll never forget the hungry look on his face. He was...gross."

I shuddered, remembering that day, and Damon tightened his grip on me. "He'd made a deal with my father that he would take me as his mate in exchange for his debt."

"Jesus." I could feel him vibrating with anger.

I blinked rapidly, fighting off tears. I'd cried my last tears over what happened years ago.

"He made all these comments about hoping I was still a virgin like my dad promised, and how he was looking forward to breaking me in. All the while, my parents just stood there, saying nothing other than that I owed it to them to help them."

"I'm going to dig up your father and kill him again, I swear to God."

I looked up and gave him a sad smile. "The fox finally went away, to give my parents some time to 'convince me'. When I got away, I went upstairs and packed all my stuff. I waited until my parents went to bed, loaded up the car that I'd bought with my wages from working at the grocery store, and drove as far as I could go. I didn't stop until I hit the Pacific Ocean. That's how I ended up in Washington."

"Fuck. I don't even know what to say to all that other than I'm so sorry you had to go through that alone."

"I called Connie from Seattle when she got back from her honeymoon. She tried to convince me to come back and move in with her and Andy, but I knew that being in Greysden put me in danger, and I didn't want to risk something happening to her or Andy because of me."

"At least you still had your sister."

"Honestly, even though we talked on the phone every couple of months, I mostly cut her off all those years. I refused to step foot in town again while my parents were alive. I never even met her son Drew until this week."

"In fairness, Connie could have gone to Seattle to see you."

I appreciated his sticking up for me. "Yeah, she offered a few times, but I pushed her away for a long time. She was with her mate, so I assumed she would be obsessed with him the way my parents were with each other. I know now that wasn't true. It was...unfair of me to assume she'd totally changed because she had a mate. Maybe some small part of me was upset that she wasn't at home to protect me from my parents and that fox. I didn't realize that until I was back here. But it's been nice to reconnect with her on this trip."

Damon shifted until he was laying over me, his weight braced on his arms. He met my eyes, and I could feel the protectiveness, regret, and love through the mate bond.

"I promise you Angie, you will never be alone again. I'd die before I let something happen to you. I also won't cage you, Mate. I want us to be equals, and to have our own lives. Most importantly, I want you to be in this willingly, not just because we lost control of our wolves."

I knew he meant it, I could feel the truth of his words through the bond.

"I'm not good at relationships," I told him. "I don't know how any of this works. I don't know if I want to move to Greysden, and I don't know if I want you to move to Seattle. It's all so sudden and confusing."

"How about we figure it out together?" he suggested. "We lost thirty years, I don't want to lose another minute being apart. It will be an adjustment for both of us, but we'll work it out. Together."

Looking into his eyes, I had to believe that we would be okay, that between us we could make it work.

I nodded. "You got yourself a deal."

Damon rolled back over and cuddled me close again. "Did you really date that guy who ran over the mailbox?"

"Yeah, we've been seeing each other casually for a couple of months."

He made a grumbling sound in his chest. "Humans," he said dismissively.

I couldn't help but smile. "You don't have anything to be jealous of, Mate. I had fun with him, but it was never going to be serious."

Damon's head whipped to the side to look at me. "Hey! You called me your mate."

He looked thrilled and the tiniest bit cocky so I couldn't help busting his chops. "It was a slip of the tongue, I didn't mean it."

"I'll show you a slip of the tongue," he grumbled, sliding down until he could shove his shoulders between my legs. And he did.

Epilogue – Damon

Six months later...

"Come on Mate, we're supposed to be at Drew and Gina's house already."

I pulled the blanket down from over my head and squinted at my mate. "No way, you wore me out this morning." My mate was insatiable, and I loved it. "Besides, they live two doors down, we see them all the time."

Angie rolled her eyes. "We need to be there. They have a big announcement, remember?"

I sat up. "Is this about Gina being pregnant? We already knew that. You smelled it at the wedding."

After we'd mated, Angie had moved to Greysden, convincing her employer to let her telework. She had to fly back to Seattle for a week every other month for meetings at the home office, but it was a fair compromise for the freedom to live here with me in Greysden.

We'd spent the last six months getting to know each other, and our love had grown every day. She'd moved into my house, and after each of us living alone for so long, living together was an adjustment, but we were figuring it out, day by day. We'd learned to give each other alone time on a regular basis, and we'd each created our own private space in the house for when we were working or needed to be alone.

Angie had worked hard to redevelop her relationships with family and old friends here in town since she'd moved back. I worked on growing my consulting business and had also reconnected with some old friends from when I lived here when I was younger. We also spent a lot of time with Connie and her family. I'd never been happier.

Even though we were mated, we'd also decided to officially tie the knot a couple of weeks ago. We'd opted for a small wedding ceremony in the park with just family and a few close friends. Both my daughters and their families had driven in from Denver, as well as several of Angie's good friends from Seattle. It was exactly what we wanted to make our mating official in the eyes of the law.

When Gina had hugged her after the ceremony, Angie had immediately scented that her niece-in-law was pregnant. Connie had also figured it out, but the sisters kept it quiet, waiting for the kids to make their own announcement when they were ready.

"I assume that's the news they want to share. It was nice of them to wait until we got back from our honeymoon."

Angie and I had taken a road trip to visit some national parks for our honeymoon. It had been a perfect trip, camping out under the stars and running our wolves until they were exhausted. We'd already agreed to do it again next year.

She walked over and pulled the blanket off me. "Come on Mister, you need to get ready."

I slipped my hand down to my cock, which was tenting my boxers. "Oh, I'm ready. Ready for you to ride my cock, little mate."

Angie blushed adorably. I loved that I could be playful with her.

"How about we kill two birds with one stone and share a shower?" she asked. "We can...release some pressure while we're in there."

I hopped out of bed. "You don't have to ask me twice."

As I followed my mate into the bathroom I sent up a small prayer of gratitude to the universe. Finding my mate again after all these years and getting a second chance was a dream come true. I couldn't wait to spend the rest of my life with the woman I loved. Just as soon as we were done in the shower...

***

Did you like this book? Show the love and leave me a review. Good reviews are like puppies, they make everyone feel happy.

Do you want to hear more about how Drew and Gina fell in love? Check out my book "Designer Wolf", available everywhere now.

Don't forget to click here[1] to join my mailing list. You'll get a FREE book and receive periodic notices about new releases and special sales. And keep reading for a special excerpt from "Wolf Doctor", now available at all major retailers.

Special Preview

Wolf Doctor: A Paranormal Romantic Comedy

Twilight. Colt's favorite time of the day.

Stripping off his clothes, he took a deep breath, inhaling the scents on the air. He broke into a run and felt his body change mid-stride. In less than thirty seconds he had transformed from man to wolf.

Muscles and bone lengthening as gray hair sprouted all over his body, almost white in some places. His sharp canine teeth extended from his thickening jaw. He felt his tail grow behind him and he wagged it happily from side to side as he increased his pace, moving so fast his paws seemed to barely touch the ground.

Colt's senses were immediately heightened. His vision was sharper, his ears taking in even the softest sound, and his nose twitched with the wonderful scents of the pristine forest.

He headed through the woods, exhilarating in the feeling of free movement. His wolf loved to run. He hadn't shifted in almost a week. Too long. He needed this. He needed to shift and let his wolf run as much as he needed oxygen or food.

Speaking of food, he could use a snack. He scented a group of hares a mile away and headed in that direction at a gallop. His paws ate up the ground as he tracked the smaller beasts, stopping occasionally to sniff the ground and pick up their trail.

There, up ahead, he saw a flash of fur. He moved quickly, ears pinned back, as his wolf took over, the ultimate predator.

He could smell the fear on the hare as it took off, running for its life. Colt pulled his gums back in a canine smile. He loved the chase. The harder the capture, the better it tasted.

He sped up, following the hare instinctively as it took a sharp turn to the side. He pounced, leaping after the hare. Suddenly his feet hit air. And then he was falling. Fast.

Oh crap. He had overshot and gone right over the edge of the bluff. He could practically feel the stupid hare laughing at him as he tumbled down the embankment, scrambling but unable to stop his downward momentum.

He whined as his body hit the road below with a heavy thump.

Before he could recover he heard the squealing of brakes and suddenly he was airborne again. He landed on the asphalt a second time, feeling bones breaking and muscles tearing. He smelled the scent of his own blood and dimly heard voices as he struggled to stay conscious.

"Oh my god Dennis, you hit that poor dog!" The woman sounded upset.

"I'm not sure that it's a dog Sandy, it might be a wolf," someone, presumably Dennis, responded.

Not a dog, his wolf snipped in his head, clearly offended.

Really, that's your top worry right now? he asked his wolf.

Like all shifters, Colt shared space in his mind with his animal. He and his wolf shared not only the same body, but also the same consciousness.

He noted dimly that the humans who had hit him had exited their truck and were watching him cautiously from where they had stopped. He thought about getting up and whined again. The pain was terrible. It was impossible to move.

"He's bleeding and he's in pain," Sandy said, her voice sounding closer. "We have to get him to the animal hospital."

"There's no way he's going to survive," Dennis answered. "Let me get my shotgun out of the truck and I'll put the poor thing out of his misery."

Colt lifted his head in alarm, although it cost him dearly. He made eye contact with the woman, trying to communicate with her. He tried to make himself look sad and unthreatening. He did not want to die on the side of the road, and he definitely did not want to be put down by some random human with a shotgun. With his luck the guy would be a bad shot and make his injuries even worse.

"NO," Sandy said firmly. "You are not shooting him Dennis. Get the tarp. We'll put him in the back and drive him to the vet."

"He's a wounded animal Sandy," Dennis argued. "He may attack us, especially if he is a wolf."

Sandy continued to hold Colt's gaze. "No, he won't," she replied. "Come on, let's get him some help."

Colt passed out, not knowing who would win their argument. He just hoped it was Sandy.

He did not feel the couple cautiously wrapping him in a tarp and dragging him up into the back of their pick-up. He didn't feel himself sliding around in the truck bed as they raced to the animal hospital. He didn't hear the people loading him onto a gurney and wheeling his large body into the hospital. Both his body and his mind were completely shut down now, blissfully blocking the pain.

Then he felt it. A jolt of happiness and peace.

He opened his eyes, staring through the pain as an angel looked down at him. The overhead light glowed behind her like a halo. Thick brown hair framed her beautiful face. Her eyes were deep brown and impossibly kind.

"What happened?" his angel asked. Her voice made him feel calm. She seemed familiar.

"I think he took a header off a cliff. I think he came rolling down from up above. Suddenly there he was, falling onto the road right in front of us," Dennis explained. "Before I could stop, I hit him with my truck. I didn't do it on purpose, he seemed to come out of nowhere."

The angel's hand dropped gently to his head, rubbing him softly between his ears. He closed his eyes again, pressing against the warmth of her hand and whining softly. He had one thought before he passed out again. *Mate!*

***

For more of Colt and Valerie's story, check out "Wolf Doctor" by Rose Bak. Available now at all major online retailers.

Other Books by Rose Bak

Boozy Book Club Series
Beach Reads
Bubbly & Billionaires
Martinis & Mysteries
The Good with Numbers Holiday Romance Series
Love Unmasked
The Thanksgiving Scrooge
Maid for Christmas
Countdown to Love
Valentine's Lottery
Bite-Sized Shifters Paranormal Romance Series
Wolf Doctor
Kat's Dog
Designer Wolf
Wolf Sheriff
Cocktail Wolf
The Oliver Boys Band Contemporary Romance Series
Until You Came Along
Rock Star Teacher
Rock Star Writer
Rock Star Neighbor
Loving the Holidays Contemporary Romance Series
Dating Santa
New Year's Steve
Independence Dave
Holidays with the Shifters Series
Santa's Claws
Bear Humbug
Jingle Bear
Silver Paws

Joy to the Wolf
Lion's Heart
The Diamond Bay Contemporary Romance Series
Brand New Penny
Fresh as a Daisy
Right as Rain
Reunited Series
Together Again
Finding My Baby
Standalones
Summer Wedding
Beach Wedding
Jessie's Girl
It's All About Relationships: Reflections on Love, Friendship, and Connection
What to Do If You Find a Cougar in Your Living Room: Self-Care in an Uncaring World

Catch up with these and other stories coming soon. Join my newsletter for more information[1] or follow my author page on your favorite retailer.

---

1. *https://storyoriginapp.com/giveaways/62ee758e-068f-11eb-904e-c373f6014fe1*

About the Author

Rose Bak has been obsessed with books since she got her first library card at age five. She is a passionate reader with an e-reader bursting with thousands of beloved books.

Although Rose enjoys writing both fiction and nonfiction, romance novels have always been her favorite guilty pleasure, both as a reader and an author. Rose's contemporary romance books focus on strong female characters over thirty-five and the alpha males who love them. Expect a lot of steam, a little bit of snark, and a guaranteed happily ever after.

Rose lives in the Pacific Northwest with her family, and special needs dogs. In addition to writing, she also teaches accessible yoga and loves music. Sadly, she has absolutely no musical talent, so she mostly sings in the shower.

Please sign up for my newsletter[1] to get a free book and keep up to date on all the Rose Bak romance news.

---

1. *https://storyoriginapp.com/giveaways/62ee758e-068f-11eb-904e-c373f6014fe1*

Don't miss out!

Visit the website below and you can sign up to receive emails whenever Rose Bak publishes a new book. There's no charge and no obligation.

https://books2read.com/r/B-A-VATM-SCLYB

BOOKS 2 READ

Connecting independent readers to independent writers.